PUFFIN BOOKS

Published by the Penguin Group
Penguin Books Ltd, 27 Wrights Lane, London W8 5TZ, England
Penguin Books USA Inc., 375 Hudson Street, New York, New York 10014, USA
Penguin Books Australia Ltd, Ringwood, Victoria, Australia
Penguin Books Canada Ltd, 10 Alcorn Avenue, Toronto, Ontario, Canada M4V 3B2
Penguin Books (NZ) Ltd, 182–190 Wairau Road, Auckland 10, New Zealand

Penguin Books Ltd, Registered Offices: Harmondsworth, Middlesex, England

First published by Reinhardt Books in association with Viking 1993
Published in Puffin Books 1996
3 5 7 9 10 8 6 4 2

Made and printed in Italy by Printers srl – Trento

Sarah Garland

What Am I Doing?

PUFFIN BOOKS
in association with Reinhardt Books Ltd

What am I climbing?

What am I riding?

What am I spying?

What am I mixing up?

What am I driving?

What am I building?

What am I ploughing?

What am I flying?

What am I racing?

What am I walking on?

What am I sailing?

Where am I going?